THE DRAGON'S SECRET:

THE CLAN BOOK 2

LEA LARSEN

© 2016

DISCLAIMER:

THE INFORMATION PRESENTED IN THIS BOOK REPRESENTS THE VIEWS OF THE PUBLISHER AS OF THE DATE OF PUBLICATION. THE PUBLISHER RESERVES THE RIGHTS TO ALTER UPDATE THEIR OPINIONS BASED ON NEW

CONDITIONS. THIS REPORT IS FOR INFORMATIONAL PURPOSES ONLY. THE AUTHOR AND THE PUBLISHER DO NOT ACCEPT ANY RESPONSIBILITIES FOR ANY LIABILITIES RESULTING FROM THE USE OF THIS INFORMATION. WHILE

EVERY ATTEMPT HAS BEEN MADE TO VERIFY THE INFORMATION PROVIDED HERE, THE AUTHOR AND THE PUBLISHER CANNOT ASSUME ANY RESPONSIBILITY FOR ERRORS, INACCURACIES OR OMISSIONS. ANY SIMILARITIES WITH PEOPLE OR FACTS ARE UNINTENTIONAL.

TABLE OF CONTENTS

Chapter One 5
Chapter Two 13
Chapter Three 19
Chapter Four 37

Chapter One

ALANA WAS GETTING MORE THAN A LITTLE SICK OF THIS LIFE OF LUXURY. SHE HAD BEEN STUCK IN THE ROOM WHERE LLEWELLYN HAD PLACED HER FOR NEARLY THREE WEEKS. IN THAT TIME, THE ONLY OTHER SOUL SHE HAD ENCOUNTERED (NOT COUNTING HER FORAY INTO THE CIRCLE OF DRAGONS ON HER FIRST DAY AT THE MANOR) WAS LLEWELLYN.

AN UNSEEN SOMEONE ALWAYS CAME INTO THE ROOM BEFORE SHE WOKE IN THE MORNING TO PROVIDE HER WITH BREAKFAST, NEW CLOTHES AND CLEAN TOWELS FOR HER BATH OR SHOWER. THE DRESSES THEY PROVIDED HER WERE ALWAYS LOVELY, SILK THINGS OR CUTE COCKTAIL DRESSES. THEY WERE ALL BEAUTIFUL AND, SHE HAD TO ADMIT, LOOKED STUNNING ON HER. BUT AFTER A WEEK OF LOUNGING AROUND IN SILK GOWNS, SHE WAS BEGINNING TO MISS SWEATPANTS AND T-SHIRTS.

LLEWELLYN CAME TO GIVE HER LUNCH AND DINNER.

IT WASN'T THAT ALANA MINDED SEEING LLEWELLYN. IN FACT, HIS VISITS HAD BECOME THE HIGHLIGHT OF HER DAY.

MUCH TO HER CHAGRIN, HE HAD NOT KISSED HER OR EVEN TRULY TOUCHED HER AGAIN SINCE THAT FIRST DAY. IN FACT, HE SEEMED TO BE AVOIDING GETTING TOO CLOSE TO HER AT ALL.

THEY TALKED, BUT HE ALWAYS MADE SURE TO KEEP A SAFE DISTANCE. INSTEAD OF SITTING NEXT TO HER ON THE WINDOW SEAT, HE WOULD PULL A CHAIR OUT FROM BESIDE THE BED. WHEN HE SAID GOOD NIGHT, HE MADE SURE TO STAND A GOOD TWO FEET FROM HER. AND, SINCE THAT VERY FIRST NIGHT, SHE HAD FELT NOTHING FROM HIM LIKE THE SEARING KISS HE HAD PLACED ON HER FOREHEAD.

SHE STILL YEARNED TO TOUCH HIM OF COURSE, TO HAVE HIM TOUCH HER. EVERY TIME HE GAVE HER THAT HALF SMILE THAT MADE HIM LOOK UNDENIABLY SEXY. EVERY TIME HE SO MUCH AS STRETCHED HIS HAND TO REACH FOR HIS GLASS SO THAT SHE COULD SEE HIS WELL-DEFINED MUSCLES IN THE TOO TIGHT T-SHIRTS HE WORE, IT WAS ALL SHE COULD DO NOT TO CROSS THE ROOM AND POUNCE ON HIM.

AND, WHAT'S MORE, SHE HAD A FEELING HE FELT THE SAME WAY ABOUT HER. SHE'D SEEN HIM LOOK HER WAY WHEN THEY SPOKE. SHE HAD SEEN THE HUNGRY GLANCE HE GAVE HER when she leaned over to speak to him. She saw him, barely, almost imperceptibly lick his lips when she stretched in her seat drawing attention to the way the dresses he'd given her clung to the curves of her body.

What she still couldn't figure out was why, if he wanted this as badly as she did—and he clearly did— he was still pushing her away.

She had a feeling that whatever it was had something to do with this ritual he had mentioned. She still hadn't gotten him to tell her anything more about what might actually happen at this ceremony. Nor was he particularly keen to talk about his full moon coronation.

Luckily for Alana, he was more than happy to talk about the rest of his life as a Draig — which, she had learned was the word they used for dragon shifter. And, this was more fascinating than she could have imagined.

"So, I guess you're sort of...born with the ability to do what you do?" she asked one day as Llewellyn sat down for lunch.

SHE WAS SITTING BESIDE THE WINDOW, ABSENTLY CHEWING ON A CREAM CHEESE AND CUCUMBER SANDWICH FROM THE TRAY HE HAD BROUGHT FOR HER. HE, AS USUAL, WAS SITTING IN A HIGH-BACKED AND UNCOMFORTABLE LOOKING CHAIR A GOOD DISTANCE AWAY FROM HER.

"THAT'S RIGHT," HE SAID. "IT'S NOT SOMETHING YOU LEARN. IT'S...SOMETHING YOU ARE."

"BUT, HOW DO THEY KNOW IF YOU HAVE IT WHEN YOU'RE BORN?" SHE ASKED.

"THE SHORT ANSWER IS, THEY DON'T," HE SAID. "THOUGH, A CHILD TO A MATED DRAIG COUPLE IS HARDLY EVER BORN WITHOUT THE ABILITY TO SHIFT. BUT, IT DOESN'T SHOW ITSELF UNTIL A FEW YEARS LATER."

"HOW OLD WERE YOU WHEN YOU STARTED?" SHE ASKED CURIOUSLY.

"I WAS THREE," HE ANSWERED. "IT CAME ON ME ALL OF A SUDDEN. I REMEMBER FEELING TERRIFIED."

"WHY?" SHE ASKED. "DIDN'T YOU SORT OF...DECIDE TO DO IT?"

HE SHOOK HIS HEAD WITH A SLIGHT CHUCKLE.

"IT DOESN'T QUITE WORK LIKE THAT," HE SAID. "SEE, WHEN WE'RE CHILDREN, WE CAN'T CONTROL IT. THE CHANGE JUST COMES UPON US WHEN WE'RE SCARED OR PARTICULARLY ANGRY."

"WHICH ONE WERE YOU?" SHE ASKED.

HE SET THE SANDWICH HE'D BEEN MUNCHING DOWN ON THE TRAY AND LOOKED AT HER THOUGHTFULLY.

"I SUPPOSE I WAS SCARED," HE SAID. "I DON'T REMEMBER MUCH. I WAS ALONE IN MY BED, IT WAS RAINING OUTSIDE. SUDDENLY, I HEARD THIS EXPLOSIVE CRACK OF THUNDER. THE NEXT THING I KNEW, I WAS FLYING ABOVE MY BED, MY NOSE WAS LONG AND RED AND THERE WERE LITTLE FLAMES SHOOTING FROM IT."

"IT'S A WONDER YOU DIDN'T BURN THE HOUSE DOWN," ALANA SAID.

"THEY WERE TOO SMALL TO CAUSE ANY REAL DAMAGE THEN," HE ANSWERED WITH A DISMISSIVE WAVE OF HIS HAND. "I WAS LUCKY THAT MY FATHER CAME IN SOON AFTER AND WAS ABLE TO CALM ME DOWN. BUT, AFTER THAT, I WASN'T ALLOWED TO LEAVE THE HOUSE FOR YEARS. NOT UNTIL I TOOK LESSONS ON CONTROL FROM MY FATHER AND PROVED TO MY PARENTS THAT I COULD MASTER IT."

"I KNOW HOW YOUR YOUNG SELF MUST HAVE FELT," SHE SAID. THERE WAS A HINT OF BITTERNESS IN HER VOICE WHICH EVEN SHE COULD HEAR. SHE MADE NO ATTEMPT TO HIDE IT.

"STUCK IN YOUR HOUSE. NOT REALLY KNOWING WHY. NOT KNOWING WHEN YOU'LL BE ALLOWED TO LEAVE."

HER EYES GLANCED ABSENTLY DOWN TO THE RUINED CASTLE. SHE KNEW THE SIGHT ALMOST BY HEART NOW. THE BRIGHT STONES SHIMMERING IN THE SUNLIGHT, THE TOWER WITH A DOORWAY AND WHO KNOWS WHAT INSIDE. BUT, SHE HAD LONG SINCE GIVEN UP THE HOPE OF EXPLORING THE STRUCTURE.

WHEN SHE TURNED BACK, LLEWELLYN WAS GAZING AT HER STEADFASTLY. SHE WONDERED IF SHE MIGHT HAVE FINALLY CONVINCED HIM OF SOMETHING. THOUGH SHE WASN'T SURE WHAT.

WHAT SHE HAD CONVINCED HIM OF WAS THE NEED FOR HER TO LEAVE THE ROOM. AT LEAST FOR THE EVENING. LLEWELLYN KNEW THAT SHE WAS RIGHT. THAT LONGING, WISTFUL EXPRESSION ON HER FACE AS SHE GLANCED OUT HER WINDOW WAS ONE THAT HE WAS ALL TOO FAMILIAR WITH. HE COULDN'T STAND TO

SEE HER LOOK LIKE THAT.

"ALANA," HE BEGAN HESITANTLY. "HOW WOULD YOU LIKE TO GO OUT TONIGHT?"

"GO WHERE?" ALANA ASKED, HER VOICE MIXED WITH HOPE AND SKEPTICISM.

"OUT TO THE CASTLE," HE SAID GESTURING TO THE WINDOW. HE FELT HIS HEART LIFT WHEN A BRIGHT, BEAMING SMILE CRAWLED ACROSS HER FACE.

"ARE YOU SURE?" SHE ASKED.

"OF COURSE, I KNOW YOU WANT TO SEE IT."

FOR HER PART, ALANA FELT HER PULSE JUMP IN HER CHEST, HER HEART POUND IN EXCITEMENT. AFTER THREE WEEKS OF NOTHING BUT READING AND TRYING ON CLOTHES; THREE WEEKS OF STARING LONGINGLY AT THE RUINED CASTLE, SHE WAS FINALLY GOING TO BE ABLE TO SEE IT. PERHAPS SHE COULD EVEN GO INTO THE TOWER. MAYBE SHE COULD CLIMB ITS HEIGHTS AND STAND AT THE TOP LOOKING OVER AT THE CLIFFS AND RIVERS ON EITHER SIDE OF THEM.

MAYBE, LLEWELLYN WOULD CLIMB IT WITH HER. THAT THOUGHT MADE HER HEART POUND

EVEN QUICKER.

"YES!" SHE SAID. "I'D LOVE TO GO OUT TONIGHT."
"WONDERFUL," HE SAID. "WE'LL LEAVE JUST AFTER DINNER."

WITH THAT, HE SAID GOODBYE AND LEFT THE ROOM. AS LLEWELLYN WALKED DOWN THE STAIRWELL, HOWEVER, HE COULD NOT HELP BUT WORRY. BEING ALONE WITH ALANA IN A ROOM HE COULD CONTROL WAS ONE THING.

HER SUITE HAD PLENTY OF SPACE AND PLENTY OF FURNITURE. HE COULD KEEP HIS DISTANCE IN THERE.

BUT, WALKING WITH HER IN THE CASTLE, GUIDING HER AROUND THE ANCIENT ROCKS, HOLDING HER HAND TO HELP HER UP THE RICKETY STAIRWAY IN THE TOWER, WAS GOING TO BE ANOTHER THING ENTIRELY.

BREATHING A SIGH, HE LEANED BACK AGAINST A WALL IN THE STAIRWELL AND PRAYED TO WHOEVER MIGHT BE LISTENING THAT HE WOULD BE ABLE TO GET THROUGH THIS NIGHT WITH HIS HEART INTACT.

Chapter Two

The evening came much more quickly than Llewellyn had expected. He'd had a tray sent up to Alana's room with dinner. Usually, he brought it himself but, tonight, he thought it might be best that he not spend more time alone with her than was absolutely necessary.

As it was, he walked out of his own room that evening and towards the stairwell that led to hers with more than a hint of trepidation. As he turned the corner to the stairwell, he was stopped in his tracks by a figure lurking in the shadow of the setting sun.

"I thought the Arefol's dinner had already been sent up."

"Owain," Llewellyn said, breathing a slight sigh of relief at the sight of his brother. "You shouldn't jump out at me like that."

"And you shouldn't be spending as much time as you are with that girl," Owain said moving towards his brother menacingly. Though Owain was not tall

OR AS MUSCULAR AS MANY OF THE MEN IN THE TRIBE, LLEWELLYN KNEW BETTER THAN TO UNDERESTIMATE HIM. HIS BROTHER WAS AS SHREWD AND CALCULATING AS ANYONE HE HAD EVER MET.

IN THAT WAY, OWAIN RESEMBLED THEIR FATHER MUCH MORE CLOSELY THAN LLEWELLYN FEARED HE EVER COULD. LLEW AND OWAIN'S FATHER KNEW HOW TO GET WHAT HE WANTED AND HE COULD BEND ANYONE TO HIS WILL.

EVEN THOUGH LLEWELLYN WAS OLDER, IT WAS CLEAR THAT OWAIN WAS MORE HIS FATHER'S SON. A FACT OWAIN POINTED OUT FREQUENTLY. A FACT THAT ALSO MADE THE YOUNGER BROTHER DESIRE THE CLAN'S THRONE FOR HIMSELF.

HIS BROTHER'S INTENTIONS WERE MADE MORE EVIDENT BY THE WAY OWAIN MOVED TOWARDS LLEW NOW. HEAD THROWN BACK, CHEST PUFFED OUT, REACHING HIS FULL HEIGHT. CLEARLY HE WAS MAKING AN ATTEMPT TO CHALLENGE LLEW'S AUTHORITY.

WELL, LLEW THOUGHT, IF HIS BROTHER WANTED TO PLAY THAT GAME, HE WOULD PLAY TOO. LLEWELLYN MOVED TOWARDS OWAIN STRETCHING TO HIS OWN FULL HEIGHT WHICH STOOD NEARLY FIVE INCHES TALLER

THAN HIS BROTHER.

"WHAT I CHOOSE TO DO WITH THE GIRL IS NONE OF YOUR CONCERN," LLEWELLYN SAID. HE LOOKED IN HIS BROTHER'S EYES AND WAITED FOR OWAIN TO BACK DOWN. TO TAKE A STEP BACKWARD, BOW HIS HEAD AND SHIFT HIS EYES TO THE FLOOR AS THE YOUNGER MAN ALWAYS HAD IN THEIR LITTLE DOMINANCE BATTLES BEFORE.

THIS TIME, OWAIN DID NOT STEP BACK. HE LOOKED LLEWELLYN SQUARE IN THE EYE.

"OUR FAMILY, OUR CLAN IS MY CONCERN," OWAIN SAID. "I WILL NOT SEE YOU DESTROY THEM."

"AND WHAT IF ALANA CAN SAVE THEM?" LLEWELLYN ASKED.

"I KNOW YOUR THEORY," OWAIN SAID. "YOU THINK WE NEED NEW BLOOD. YOU THINK THAT WILL HELP US. IT WON'T. IF YOU MATE WITH THIS GIRL, YOU'LL DILUTE OUR BLOOD. WE WILL DIE OUT MORE QUICKLY THAN WE ARE NOW."
"YOU CAN'T KNOW THAT," LLEWELLYN SAID.

"I KNOW ENOUGH," OWAIN ANSWERED. "THIS LITTLE GIRL HAS TURNED YOUR HEAD. YOU THINK THAT, BECAUSE YOU DESIRE HER, YOU

SHOULD BE ABLE TO MATE HER. NEVER MIND WHAT IT MIGHT MEAN FOR THE CLAN. FOR YOUR FAMILY."

HE'D GROWN TIRED OF THIS GAME. HE HAD HEARD ALL HIS BROTHER'S ARGUMENTS AGAINST TAKING AN AREFOL MATE BEFORE. HE DIDN'T CARE TO LISTEN AGAIN. KEEPING HIS EYES ON HIS BROTHER, HE PUSHED PAST HIM TO MOVE UP THE STAIRS.

IT WAS ONLY WHEN LLEW TURNED AROUND TO ASCEND THE STAIRCASE THAT OWAIN SPOKE AGAIN.

"I CAN STOP YOU FROM MATING HER."

LLEWELLYN STOPPED DEAD IN HIS TRACKS WHEN HIS BROTHER'S VOICE CARRIED UP THE STAIRWELL. HIS BLOOD BEGAN TO RUN COLD AS HE TURNED AGAIN TO FACE THE YOUNGER MAN. WHEN HE DID, HIS BROTHER WAS WEARING A SUPERIOR SMIRK THAT LLEWELLYN KNEW ALL TOO WELL.

"ALL THE SACRED TEXTS SAY YOU NEED A VIRGIN FOR A MATE," OWAIN SAID. "WHAT IF I WERE TO PAY THE AREFOL A LITTLE VISIT IN HER ROOM TONIGHT?"

"YOU WOULDN'T DARE," LLEWELLYN SAID. HIS VOICE CAME OUT AS A LOW GROWL WITHOUT

HIS WILL OR APPROVAL.

"I WOULD," OWAIN SAID. THE SMILE FADING FROM HIS FACE. "I WOULD DO THAT AND MORE TO SAVE MY FAMILY. I WONDER IF YOU CAN SAY THE SAME."

IN A FLASH, LLEWELLYN LAUNCHED HIMSELF DOWN THE STAIRS. BEFORE HE WAS FULLY AWARE OF HIMSELF, HE FOUND THAT HE HAD PUSHED HIS BROTHER AGAINST THE WALL OF THE HALLWAY. HIS ARMS PINNING HIM TO THE HARD SURFACE.

"IF YOU SO MUCH AS TOUCH HER," LLEWELLYN GROWLED, HIS FACE MERE INCHES FROM OWAIN'S. "I SWEAR, I WILL KILL YOU. FAMILY OR NOT."

OWAIN LOOKED BACK AT LLEWELLYN DEFIANTLY FOR A MOMENT BEFORE LOWERING HIS HEAD AND AVERTING HIS GAZE IN SUBMISSION. AS SOON AS HE DID, LLEWELLYN RELEASED HIS HOLD ON HIS BROTHER AND ALLOWED HIM TO WALK AWAY.

"WELL THEN," LLEWELLYN SAID AS HE REACHED THE HALLWAY ENTRANCE. "I SUPPOSE I'VE GOT MY ANSWER."

LLEW SAW JUST A HINT OF THAT HORRIBLE, SUPERIOR SMIRK CROSS HIS BROTHER'S FACE BEFORE THE YOUNGER MAN TURNED THE CORNER AND DISAPPEARED.

Chapter Three

ALANA PACED THE SPACE BETWEEN THE WINDOW SEAT AND HER BED ANXIOUSLY. SHE'D ALREADY DONE HER MAKE-UP, SPRITZED HERSELF WITH AN ASSORTMENT OF PERFUMES LLEW HAD SET OUT FOR HER IN THE RESTROOM AND CHECKED HER HAIR TWICE.

SHE'D REMEMBERED FEELING THIS WAY ON NEARLY EVERY FIRST DATE SHE HAD EVER BEEN ON. THE FRETTING, THE EXCITED ANTICIPATION WERE ALL THE SAME. THE ONLY DIFFERENCE WAS, THIS WAS NOT A DATE. NOT REALLY.

THE TRUTH WAS, SHE WASN'T SURE WHAT SHE WAS TO LLEW AND, WHAT'S MORE, SHE HAD NO IDEA WHAT HE EXPECTED HER TO BE. SOMETIMES, THE WAY THEY TALKED, IT WAS AS THOUGH THEY WERE DATING. BUT, OTHER TIMES, SHE FELT AS THOUGH THEY WERE BARELY FRIENDS.

SOMEHOW, SHE KNEW IT ALL HUNG ON THIS MYSTERIOUS RITUAL THAT HE REFUSED TO TELL HER ABOUT. WELL, SHE WASN'T PUTTING UP WITH THAT ANYMORE. SHE WAS GOING TO GET THE TRUTH ABOUT THIS "RITUAL" OUT OF HIM TONIGHT IF IT WAS THE LAST THING SHE

DID.

WHEN A KNOCK SOUNDED ON HER DOOR, SHE JUMPED AND, WITH AN EXCITED LITTLE BOUNCE MOVED TO ANSWER IT.

"YOU LOOK BEAUTIFUL," LLEWELLYN SAID AS SOON AS HE CAUGHT SIGHT OF HER. SHE COULDN'T HELP BUT BLUSH AS HE TOOK IN THE RED COCKTAIL DRESS AND FLAT BALLET SLIPPERS SHE'D CHOSEN FOR THE OCCASION.

"I GUESS IT'S NOT GREAT FOR SCALING ANCIENT RUINS," SHE SAID. "BUT, THEN AGAIN, NOTHING IN MY WARDROBE IS."

SHE REALIZED TOO LATE THAT HE MIGHT TAKE THAT AS AN INSULT TO HIS TASTE IN CLOTHING. AFTER ALL, SHE SUPPOSED IT WAS LLEWELLYN WHO WAS PICKING OUT HER BEAUTIFUL WARDROBE. THE LAST THING SHE WANTED TO DO WAS MAKE HIM THINK SHE WAS UNGRATEFUL.

LUCKILY FOR ALANA, LLEWELLYN DID NOT THINK ANYTHING OF THE SORT. IN FACT, HE WAS TOO TAKEN IN BY THE WAY THE RED DRESS HUGGED HER CURVES PERFECTLY, STOPPING JUST AT THE KNEE. THE WAY THE SKIN ON HER NECK GLEAMED IN THE LIGHT OF THE SETTING SUN MOVING THROUGH THE WINDOW. SO SOFT HE COULD ALMOST REACH

OUT AND TOUCH IT.

"YOU'RE PERFECT," HE SAID AND MEANT IT. THOUGH, HE REALIZED THAT IF HE WAS TO AVOID THE VERY PITFALLS HE FEARED, HE SHOULD STOP STARING AT HER.

"SHALL WE GO?" HE ASKED.

SHE NODDED AND HE LEAD HER DOWN THE STAIRWELL AND OUT THROUGH THE BACK DOOR.

ALANA HAD COME OUT THIS WAY ONCE BEFORE. WHEN SHE DISCOVERED WHAT LLEW TRULY WAS. THOUGH, ON THAT DAY, SHE HAD BEEN FORCED TO CREEP OUTSIDE AS QUIETLY AS SHE COULD. AND, HER MIND HAD BEEN SO FILLED WITH MEN SHIFTING INTO DRAGONS THAT THERE HAD BEEN VERY LITTLE ROOM FOR ANYTHING ELSE.

NOW, THIS SPOT SEEMED DIFFERENT. GREENER. SAFER, SHE SUPPOSED, NOW THAT LLEW HAD GRABBED HOLD OF HER HAND AND WAS GUIDING HER TO THE RUINS OF THE ANCIENT CASTLE.

"IT'S SO BEAUTIFUL HERE," SHE SAID.

"I SUPPOSE IT IS," HE ANSWERED.

"YOU SUPPOSE?"

"I'VE NEVER BEEN ANYWHERE ELSE," HE SAID WITH A SHRUG. "SO, I CAN'T REALLY MAKE AN INFORMED DECISION."

"YOU'VE NEVER BEEN OUTSIDE OF WALES?" SHE ASKED, HER EYES NARROWING IN CURIOSITY. HE SHOOK HIS HEAD 'NO'.

"TOO DANGEROUS," HE SAID. "EVEN THOUGH I CAN CONTROL MY SHIFTING NOW, THERE'S NO TELLING WHAT MIGHT HAPPEN ALONE ON THE ROAD. WHEN WE DO TRAVEL, WE GO IN PAIRS OR GROUPS. AND, IT'S ALMOST ALWAYS ON SOME MISSION FOR THE CLAN."

"LIKE THE ONE IN CARDIFF?" SHE ASKED.

HE NODDED 'YES'. WHEN THEY STOPPED AT ONE OF THE LARGER STONES, HE LOOKED OUT TOWARDS THE SETTING SUN BEHIND THE CLIFFS IN THE WEST. THE EXPRESSION HE WORE WAS ONE OF SAD DESPERATION. ALMOST AS THOUGH HE WAS TRAPPED.

SHE KNEW THE FEELING WELL. THOUGH, ODDLY, NOW THAT SHE WAS HERE, NOT IN HER ROOM, BUT ROAMING A RUIN WITH LLEWELLYN BY HER SIDE, SHE DIDN'T FEEL TRAPPED ANYMORE. IN FACT, SHE FELT FREER THAN SHE HAD EVER FELT IN HER LIFE.

ALANA CLOSED HER EYES AND LEANED AGAINST ONE OF THE STANDING STONES THAT HAD ONCE MADE UP THE CASTLE WALL. SHE LISTENED TO THE RUSH OF THE SMALL CREEK JUST DOWN THE HILL, FELT THE BREEZE ON HER FACE AND THOUGHT, FOR THE FIRST TIME SINCE SHE HAD LEFT AMERICA, SHE MAY HAVE FOUND A PLACE WHERE SHE COULD BELONG.

"IS THERE ANYTHING YOU WANTED TO SEE IN PARTICULAR?" LLEWELLYN ASKED, CAUSING HER TO OPEN HER EYES.
"YES," SHE ANSWERED, SUDDENLY REMEMBERING THE ONE THING SHE HAD BEEN THE MOST CURIOUS ABOUT. "COULD WE CLIMB TO THE TOP OF THE TOWER."

LLEWELLYN SMILED AND OFFERED HER HIS HAND AS HE LED HER TO THE ANCIENT STONE ARCHWAY THAT HAD ONCE HELD A DOOR. HE LED HER UP THE STAIRS HEARING HER SMALL FOOTSTEPS ECHO AGAINST THE ROCKS.

FINALLY, THEY REACHED THE TOP OF THE TOWER AND LOOKED OUT TO THE MOUNTAINS AND CLIFFS BEYOND.

THE SUN HAD NEARLY SET NOW, CASTING THE SUN IN A MIXTURE OF ORANGE, YELLOW, PURPLE AND PINK HUES.

"WOW," SHE WHISPERED, RUSHING TOWARDS THE EDGE OF THE TOWER.

LLEWELLYN HEARD HER GASP ONCE AGAIN AS SHE LEANED OVER AND LOOKED DOWN AT THE VALLEY BELOW THEM.

"I FEEL LIKE I CAN SEE THE WORLD FROM HERE," SHE SAID.

"WE CAN SEE A WORLD," HE SAID. "AND, THAT'S ALWAYS BEEN ENOUGH FOR ME."

SHE DIDN'T ANSWER BUT CONTINUED TO SURVEY THE GROUND BELOW, FINALLY, HER EYES CAME TO REST ON A LARGE CIRCLE OF STONES IN THE MIDDLE OF THE CASTLE RUIN. SHE WOULD HAVE DISMISSED IT AS YET ANOTHER SIGN OF DECAY IF THESE PARTICULAR STONES HAD NOT BEEN PLACED SO DELIBERATELY.

"WHAT ARE THOSE?" SHE ASKED POINTING TO THE STONES AND LOOKING TO LLEWELLYN.

HE DID NOT ANSWER RIGHT AWAY. HE WAS THINKING HOW BEST TO TELL HER. HE KNEW HE HAD TO AT SOME POINT. IT ONLY MADE SENSE TO DO IT HERE. NOW THAT SHE WAS HAPPIER AND OUT OF THE HOUSE.
STILL, HE TOOK A LARGE PAINFUL BREATH BEFORE SAYING.

"THAT IS WHERE THE RITUAL...THE CORONATION WILL TAKE PLACE NEXT WEEK."

"AH, IS THAT WHAT THIS MYSTERIOUS RITUAL IS? A CORONATION?" SHE ASKED IN A TEASING VOICE. THE FLIRTY SMILE SHE GAVE HIM ONLY SERVED TO TWIST HIS HEART MORE PAINFULLY. HOW COULD HE TELL HER ABOUT THE CHOICE SHE WOULD HAVE TO MAKE? HOW COULD HE TELL HER WHAT WAS AT STAKE FOR HIS FAMILY? HIS CLAN?

WELL, HE SUPPOSED, IT WAS BEST TO START AT THE BEGINNING.

"THERE'S MORE TO IT THAN THAT," HE SAID. "DURING THIS RITUAL, I WILL BE OFFICIALLY MADE LEADER OF THE CLAN. AND, WHEN I AM MADE LEADER, I MUST CHOOSE A MATE."

"A MATE?" SHE ASKED. THOUGH SHE HAD TO ADMIT, SHE ALREADY HAD A GOOD IDEA WHAT THAT MIGHT MEAN.

"A...A WIFE, I SUPPOSE YOU WOULD CALL IT," HE SAID. "ONCE THE WOMAN I CHOOSE AND I ARE MATED, WE ARE BOUND FOR LIFE. IT'S A SACRED BOND THAT WE CAN NOT BREAK."

"I SEE," SHE SAID. SO, LLEWELLYN WANTED HER TO BE HIS...WIFE? IT WAS OVERWHELMING

SURELY. BUT, SHE DISCOVERED, THE IDEA CAUSED A SMILE TO CREEP ACROSS HER FACE. IT CAUSED HER HEART TO FLUTTER MORE IN EXCITEMENT THAN ANXIETY.

"THAT'S NOT ALL," HE SAID. "WHEN I CHOOSE A MATE, WE WILL HAVE TO...CONSUMMATE OUR RELATIONSHIP IN FRONT OF THE WITNESSES AT THE RITUAL."

"YOU MEAN YOU'LL HAVE TO HAVE YOUR...WEDDING NIGHT...IN FRONT OF AN AUDIENCE?" SHE ASKED.

"ESSENTIALLY, YES," HE SAID.

WELL, THAT DID MAKE THINGS MORE COMPLICATED. AND, AS MUCH AS SHE LOVED TALKING IN HYPOTHETICALS, IT WAS ABOUT TIME, SHE THOUGHT THAT THEY SPOKE FRANKLY ABOUT HER ROLE IN ALL OF THIS.

"AND...I GUESS...THAT'S WHY YOU BROUGHT ME HERE?" SHE ASKED TIMIDLY.

"YES AND NO," HE SAID SOUNDING RELUCTANT. HER EYES NARROWED AND A CONFUSED FROWN LINED HER LIPS.

"YOU SEE BECAUSE YOU ARE...NOT ONE OF OUR CLAN," HE SAID. "MY BROTHER AND SEVERAL OF THE OTHERS THINK YOU WOULD MAKE A

BETTER...CONSORT THAN A MATE."

"CONSORT?" SHE ASKED. THOUGH, SHE HAD A FEELING THAT THIS WAS WHAT SHE HAD HEARD LLEW, HIS BROTHER, AND THEIR MOTHER DISCUSS THE NIGHT SHE WAS BROUGHT TO THE MANOR.

"YOU SEE," HE SAID. "SINCE WE HAVE SO FEW WOMEN, THE MEN IN OUR CLAN NEED TO RELEASE THEIR URGES. IN AGES BEFORE, WE'VE USED NON-CLAN MEMBERS AS CONSORTS TO...FULFILL THOSE NEEDS."

"SO, I WOULD BE A PROSTITUTE?" SHE ASKED. THOUGH SHE KNEW THAT WASN'T EXACTLY THE TERM FOR IT. SEX SLAVE WOULD BE MORE ACCURATE.

"IF YOU WERE TO BE MADE A CONSORT," HE SAID. "YOU WOULD BE STERILIZED SO THAT YOU COULD NOT HAVE CHILDREN. THEN, YOU WOULD BE AT THE MERCY OF EVERY MAN IN THE CLAN WHENEVER HE WANTED YOU. DAY OR NIGHT."

THE HORROR OF THAT FILLED HER IRREVOCABLY. SO MUCH SO THAT SHE LOOKED DOWN AT THE GROUND AND FELT TEARS BEGINNING TO WELL UP IN HER EYES.

"ALANA," LLEWELLYN SAID SOFTLY. HE

touched her chin and brought her gaze up to meet his. "Please, know that is not what I want for you."

"Then the only other option," Alana said, swallowing hard and looking into his eyes. "Is to...consummate my relationship with you...in front of potentially hostile witnesses."

"I know it's not ideal," he said. "And, if...if that is not what you want either. If you don't want to be my mate...I suppose I could find a way to sneak you out of the manor. But, you should be warned that the clan will likely find you, no matter where you go, and I can't protect you out there."

She nodded and pulled away from him moving to the edge of the tower again. Her mind spinning. She had dreamed, for weeks of Llew taking her, of him dominating her, making her his.

Now, she had the opportunity. And, what's more, he seemed to want that from her as well. But...it would be her first time. In front of an audience. What if she faltered? What if she wasn't any good at it?

STILL, WHEN SHE THOUGHT OF THE ALTERNATIVES...THEY WERE BOTH TOO HORRIBLE TO IMAGINE. EITHER LIVE LIFE AS A SLAVE TO DOZENS OF MEN OR LEAVE LLEW AND THE BEAUTY OF THIS PLACE BEHIND FOREVER.

"ALANA," LLEW SAID SOFTLY, COMING UP BEHIND HER. SHE LET OUT A SHARP BREATH WHEN HE PUT A GENTLE HAND ON HER SHOULDER. "WHAT ARE YOU THINKING?"

AS THE LAST LIGHT FROM THE SUN FADED BEHIND A LARGE MOUNTAIN TO THE WEST, SHE TURNED TO HIM, BARELY MAKING OUT HIS FACE IN THE DARKNESS.

"I THINK," SHE BEGAN SLOWLY. "THAT GIVEN THE CHOICE OF SEX SLAVE OR SEX WITH A GORGEOUS MAN IN FRONT OF AN AUDIENCE, I'LL TAKE THE LATTER."

HE LOOKED AT HER A LONG MOMENT AS THOUGH UNABLE TO BELIEVE WHAT SHE HAD JUST SAID. THEN, SLOWLY, A SMILE CREPT OVER HIS FACE.

"BESIDES," SHE SAID, SMILING AT HIM IN TURN. "I DON'T WANT TO LEAVE HERE. IT'S THE FIRST PLACE I'VE REALLY FELT AT HOME IN, FOR YEARS."

"WELL, I'M GLAD OF THAT," HE SAID. "NOW, IT'S DARK. WE SHOULD GO INSIDE."

HE OFFERED HER HIS HAND WHICH SHE GRATEFULLY TOOK AND HE BEGAN TO LEAD HER DOWN THE TOWER STEPS AND OUT INTO THE RUIN.

AS THEY MADE THEIR WAY TO THE BACK DOOR, LLEWELLYN FOUND THAT HE COULD NOT KEEP THE SMILE FROM HIS FACE. SHE WAS GOING TO BE HIS MATE. THIS GIRL. THIS AMAZING, BEAUTIFUL, INTELLIGENT YOUNG WOMAN WAS GOING TO BE HIS FOREVER.

KNOWING THIS, IT WAS ALL HE COULD DO NOT TO WRAP HER IN HIS ARMS AND TAKE HER RIGHT THERE, RITUAL AND TRADITION BE DAMNED. HER SMALL HAND IN HIS AS THEY CLIMBED THE STAIRS AND THE SIGHT OF HER BACK IN THAT RED DRESS AS A LONG DARK BRAID CASCADED DOWN HER BACK DID NOTHING TO WEAKEN HIS DESIRE.

WHEN THEY REACHED HER ROOM, SHE TURNED TO HIM AND SMILED.
"THANK YOU FOR TONIGHT," SHE SAID. "I NEEDED IT."

"I KNOW," HE ANSWERED. TRYING TO KEEP HIS SENSES FROM FILLING WITH THE SCENT OF HER PERFUME. "I THINK WE BOTH DID."

SHE SMILED AGAIN AND HIS HEART STOPPED AS SHE REACHED UP ON HER TOES AND GAVE HIM A SOFT, LINGERING KISS ON HIS CHEEK. THE WARMTH OF HER LIPS AGAINST HIS SKIN, THE SCENT OF HER PERFUME, CAUSED HIM TO LOSE ALL RESOLVE.

BEFORE HE KNEW WHAT HE WAS DOING, HE GRABBED HOLD OF HER SHOULDERS, PUSHED HER INTO THE ROOM AND CLOSED THE DOOR BEFORE PRESSING HIS LIPS DESPERATELY AGAINST HERS.

ALANA FELT HIS MEMBER PRESS AGAINST HER LEG THROUGH THE THIN FABRIC OF HER DRESS AS LLEWELLYN SHOVED HER AGAINST THE HARD WOOD OF THE DOOR.

THERE WAS NOTHING AT ALL SOFT OR GENTLE ABOUT THIS KISS. HIS TONGUE PUSHED FORCEFULLY INSIDE HER MOUTH AS THOUGH HE WAS TRYING TO INVADE HER VERY SOUL. SHE MOANED WHEN SHE FELT ONE OF HIS HANDS MOVE UP TO HER BREAST JUST AS HIS LIPS BIT AND SUCKED THE SKIN AT HER NECK.

HE NIBBLED AT HER JAWLINE BEFORE BRINGING HIS LIPS UP TO TRACE THE OUTSIDE OF HER EAR.

"DO YOU HAVE ANY IDEA WHAT YOU DO TO

ME, ALANA?" HE ASKED. "DO YOU KNOW HOW LONG I'VE WANTED TO GRAB YOU AND FUCK YOU UNTIL YOU FORGET EVERYTHING ELSE?"

A SURGE OF MOISTURE FLOODED TO HER CORE AS SHE REVELED IN THE FEEL OF HIS HANDS RUNNING UP AND DOWN HIS TORSO. SUDDENLY, SHE KNEW SHE WANTED TO BE MUCH MORE ACTIVE IN THIS PROCESS, AS INEXPERIENCED AS SHE WAS, SHE KNEW THAT LLEW WOULD TEACH HER.
HESITANTLY, SHE REACHED HER HAND TO THE CROTCH OF HIS TROUSERS AND COVERED HIS MEMBER.

THE LOW MOAN HE LET OUT GAVE HER A LITTLE SWELL OF VICTORY. SHE REACHED UP BEHIND HIS NECK AND GAVE HIM A BRIEF KISS BEFORE MOVING HER LIPS TO HIS EAR.

"WHY DON'T YOU SHOW ME?" SHE ASKED.

WITH ANOTHER GROWL, HE PUSHED HER BACK AGAINST THE DOOR AS HER HAND CONTINUED TO STROKE THE MEMBER STILL GROWING BENEATH HIS TROUSERS.
LLEWELLYN, MOVED HIS OWN HAND UNDERNEATH HER DRESS TO TOUCH HER DESIRE THROUGH HER PANTIES. EVEN OVER THE FABRIC HE COULD FEEL HOW WARM AND WET SHE WAS.

AND IT WAS ALL FOR HIM. SHE BELONGED TO HIM.

NO, WAIT. THAT WASN'T RIGHT. SHE WOULD BELONG TO HIM. BUT, SHE DID NOT YET. SHE COULDN'T UNTIL THE RITUAL. THE OTHER MEMBERS OF THE CLAN WOULD KNOW IF SHE WAS NOT A VIRGIN WHEN HE TOOK HER THE NIGHT OF THE FULL MOON. THEY WOULD SENSE IT AS HE HAD WHEN HE FIRST MET HER.

IF THEY DID, THERE WAS NO TELLING WHAT THEY MIGHT DO.

ONCE AGAIN, THIS DESPERATE PLEASURE WAS BROUGHT TO AN END BY THE SOBERING THOUGHT OF DUTY. HE TOOK HIS HAND AWAY FROM HER CENTER AND GRABBED HOLD OF HER WRIST, PRYING IT FROM HIS OWN MEMBER. STILL PAINFULLY ERECT INSIDE HIS PANTS.

"WHAT IS IT?" SHE ASKED AS HE PULLED AWAY FROM HER.

"I'VE TOLD YOU," LLEWELLYN SAID. "WE CAN'T."

"WHY CAN'T WE?" SHE DEMANDED. "LLEW...DON'T YOU SEE...I WANT THIS! I WANT TO BE MATED TO YOU!"

THAT, VERY NEARLY, BROKE HIS RESOLVE. HEARING THOSE WORDS FROM HER, THAT SHE WANTED HIM JUST AS MUCH AS HE WANTED HER, WERE LIKE A THOUSAND APHRODISIACS AT ONCE.

SHE REACHED UP ON HER TOES AGAIN AND PULLED HIM DOWN FOR ANOTHER KISS. IT TOOK ALL THE STRENGTH HE HAD IN HIM TO PUSH HER AWAY ONCE AGAIN.

"NOT YET," HE WHISPERED MOVING CLOSER TO HER. GENTLY, HE TOOK HER FACE IN HIS HANDS AND PLACED A SEARING KISS ON HER FOREHEAD. JUST AS HE HAD DONE HER FIRST NIGHT AT THE MANOR.

HE BACKED OUT OF THE ROOM WITH HIS EYES STILL LOCKED ON HER. HE DIDN'T TAKE HIS EYES OFF HER FORM UNTIL HE TURNED TO MOVE DOWN THE STAIRWELL.

AS SOON AS HE WAS GONE, ALANA CLOSED THE DOOR AS LOUDLY AS SHE COULD IN HER FRUSTRATION. SHE DRESSED AND READIED HERSELF FOR BED HOPING AGAINST HOPE THAT THE ROUTINE OF THOSE ACTIONS WOULD CHASE AWAY THOUGHTS OF LLEW. WOULD FEND OFF THE AROUSAL STILL STIRRING INSIDE OF HER.

IT DIDN'T. EVEN WHEN SHE SLID INTO BED, SHE

COULDN'T HELP BUT REMEMBER THE FEELING OF HIS WARM LIPS AGAINST HER SKIN. HIS SMOOTH HANDS AGAINST HER BARE SHOULDERS, THE SOUND OF HIS VOICE IN HER EAR. THE HEAT FROM HIS SKIN AS HE TOUCHED HER ALMOST WHERE SHE DESPERATELY NEEDED TO FEEL HIM.

WITHOUT THINKING, SHE REACHED HER HAND UP HER NIGHTGOWN AS SHE RETRACED THE STEPS LLEWELLYN'S HANDS HAD TAKEN NOT ONE HOUR BEFORE. WHEN SHE CLOSED HER EYES, SHE IMAGINED WHAT MIGHT HAVE HAPPENED IF HE HADN'T STOPPED.

SHE IMAGINED HIM TAKING THOSE FIRM FINGERS AND SEEKING OUT THE VERY CENTER OF HER DESIRE. BENEATH THE COVERS, EYES STILL CLOSED, SHE DID JUST THAT. SHE LET OUT A SMALL GASP OF PLEASURE AS HER FINGERS FOUND HER CENTER AND SHE FORCED HER EYES TO REMAIN CLOSED, IMAGINING LLEWELLYN'S HAND IN PLACE OF HER OWN.

SHE IMAGINED HIM PRESSING HER HARD AGAINST THE WALL OF THIS BEDROOM AND SHOVING BOTH OF HIS FINGERS INSIDE HER. SHE LET OUT A SMALL, SHARP CRY AS HER OWN FINGERS FOLLOWED THE INSTRUCTION OF THE IMAGE IN HER MIND.

SHE IMAGINED HIM REPLACING HIS FINGERS

WITH THE LONG SLENDER COCK SHE HAD FELT BENEATH HIS TROUSERS. SHE IMAGINED HIM TOSSING HER ON THE BED AND POUNDING IN AND OUT OF HER SO QUICKLY THAT SHE BARELY HAD TIME TO BREATHE.

AS IT WAS, TENSION WAS BUILDING INSIDE OF HER; IT WAS ALL SHE COULD DO NOT TO SCREAM OUT FULLY INTO THE ROOM. STILL, SHE KEPT HER EYES CLOSED AS SHE IMAGINED THE SOUND OF HIS VOICE. HIS WARM, SWEET BREATH TICKLING HER EAR.
"COME FOR ME, ALANA," HE SAID IN HER MIND. "LET ME HEAR YOU."

"OH, GOD! LLEW!" SHE CALLED OUT INTO THE ROOM.

AS SHE CAME DOWN FROM HER ECSTASY, RAGGED AND SPENT, SHE COULD ONLY PRAY THAT NO ONE NEARBY HAD HEARD HER EMBARRASSING EXCLAMATION.

AND, AS SHE TURNED OUT HER LIGHT FOR BED, SHE KNEW THAT THE RITUAL NEXT WEEK COULD NOT COME SOON ENOUGH.

Chapter Four

SLEEP BROUGHT NO RELIEF FROM THOUGHTS OF LLEWELLYN. HE WANDERED IN AND OUT OF HER DREAMS LIKE A CORPOREAL SPIRIT. SHE WOULD FEEL HIS HANDS TOUCHING HER, HIS MOUTH ON HERS, HIS BREATH AGAINST HER NECK.

AT ONE POINT, THE DREAM BECAME SO VIVID THAT SHE WAS CERTAIN SHE WAS NOT DREAMING AT ALL. THIS WAS CONFIRMED WHEN SHE OPENED HER EYES AND FOUND HERSELF VERY MUCH AWAKE IN HER OWN ROOM.

AWAKE, WITH A MAN'S HAND MOVING SLOWLY DOWN HER CHEST AND A LARGE FIGURE LOOMING OVER HER.

"LLEW?" SHE ASKED HAZILY TO THE ROOM.

THE FIGURE BENT DOWN CLOSE ENOUGH THAT HIS FACE COULD BE SEEN IN THE FAINT BEAMS OF THE MOONLIGHT.

DARK, UNFAMILIAR EYES SHONE DOWN ON HER FROM INSIDE A FACE WHICH SHE BARELY RECOGNIZED. IT TOOK A MOMENT FOR HER TO REALIZE WHAT SHE WAS SEEING.

THE FIGURE WAS CERTAINLY NOT LLEW. ALANA OPENED HER MOUTH TO SCREAM, TO CALL OUT TO THE REST OF THE HOUSE BUT, AS SOON AS SHE DID, THIS STRANGELY FAMILIAR FIGURE PUT A FIRM HAND AGAINST HER MOUTH.

"ONE SCREAM AND I WILL SNAP YOUR NECK," THE DARK VOICE SAID OMINOUSLY.

IT WAS ONLY AFTER HE SPOKE THAT ALANA WAS TRULY ABLE TO PLACE THE MAN BEFORE HER. THIS WAS OWAIN, LLEWELLYN'S BROTHER.

SHE SAW HIM SMILE IN THE BEAMS OF THE MOONLIGHT WHICH, FOR SOME REASON, LOOKED BRIGHTER THAN THEY HAD BEEN BEFORE. SHE TURNED HER HEAD AS MUCH AS THE HAND ON HER MOUTH ALLOWED AND SAW THAT HER WINDOW HAD BEEN THROWN OPEN. NO DOUBT THAT WAS HOW THE INTRUDER HAD MADE HIS WAY INTO HER ROOM.
HIS SUPERIOR SMIRK STILL PRESENT, OWAIN'S HAND CONTINUED HIS PATH DOWN THE FRONT OF HER NIGHTDRESS. WHEN HE DIPPED BENEATH HER CLOTHES, ALANA INSTINCTIVELY BEGAN TO KICK AND CRY OUT INTO HIS HAND.

HER CRIES BECAME SHARPER WHEN HE

TOUCHED HER THROUGH HER PANTIES. "I SEE YOU'VE ALREADY STARTED," HE SAID IN A HORRIBLE, CONDESCENDING VOICE WHEN HE TOUCHED THE WARM WET SUBSTANCE STILL PRESENT IN HER UNDERWEAR.

WHEN HE FORCED A HAND INSIDE HER UNDERWEAR AND REACHED HER FOLDS, ALANA GASPED AND GAVE AN INSTINCTIVE KICK WITH HER LEG. IT CAUGHT HIM IN HIS SHIN WHICH CAUSED HIM TO TAKE THE HAND OFF HER MOUTH.

"HELP!" SHE SCREAMED INSTANTLY AS SHE ROLLED OUT FROM UNDER HIM AND JUMPED FROM THE BED. "SOMEONE HELP ME!"

"GET BACK HERE, AREFOL WHORE," HE GROWLED.

SHE FELT HER HAIR BEING YANKED BACK AND SCREAMED FULL INTO THE ROOM AS SHE WAS THROWN DOWN HARD ONTO THE FLOOR. HE WAS ON TOP OF HER ALMOST IMMEDIATELY, GRABBING HER NIGHT DRESS AND PULLING IT UP OVER HER THIGHS.

"NO ONE'S GOING TO THINK OF MATING YOU AFTER THIS," HE SAID BRINGING A HAND TO HIS OWN TROUSERS AND BEGINNING TO UNBUTTON THEM.

ANOTHER BANG SOUNDED FROM THE DOOR OF HER ROOM. AND, IN A FLASH, A LARGER PAIR OF ARMS SNAKED THEIR WAY AROUND OWAIN'S CHEST AND YANKED HIM AWAY FROM HER.

AS LLEWELLYN PULLED HIS BROTHER TO HIS FEET, HE SAW THEIR MOTHER RUSH OVER TO ALANA WHOSE NIGHT DRESS HAD BEEN TORN IN ONE STRATEGIC SPOT AND WAS NOW SPORTING A BRUISE ON HER ARM.

WHEN THE GIRL LOOKED UP AT LLEWELLYN, TEARS IN HER EYES AND A LOOK OF UTTER SHAME ON HER FACE, HE FELT SOMETHING COME OVER HIM THAT HE HAD NOT FELT IN A LONG TIME.

HE TURNED BACK TO HIS BROTHER AND AN ANGER HE COULD NOT POSSIBLY CONTROL WELLED UP INSIDE OF HIM.

ALANA SCREAMED FOR THE THIRD TIME THAT NIGHT AS THE FULLY FORMED RED DRAGON BEGAN TEARING THROUGH HER BEDROOM.

"GET DOWN," THE WOMAN NEXT TO ALANA SAID, "AS FAR AS YOU CAN." SHE FELT A PUSH AS THE WOMAN SHOVED HER UNDERNEATH THE BED. AS SHE DID, ALANA HEARD THE SOUND OF GLASS BREAKING AND GROWLS AND ANIMAL'S SCREAMS.

WHEN SHE DARED TO PEEK OUT ONCE MORE, SHE REALIZED THAT THERE WERE NOW TWO DRAGON'S, ONE SLIGHTLY SMALLER THAN THE FIRST, LOCKED IN A FEARSOME BATTLE.

WHEN THE LARGEST RED ONE SWIPED AT THE SMALLER DRAGON'S WING, THE SMALLER BEAST LET OUT A HORRIBLE SCREECH OF PAIN. THE NEXT MOMENT, THE TAIL OF THE LARGE DRAGON FLICKED SO FIERCELY THAT IT SENT HER ENTIRE BOOKSHELF FLYING OUT THE OPEN WINDOW.

ANOTHER FIERCE TAIL FLICK FROM THE LARGE DRAGON CAUGHT THE SMALL ONE DIRECTLY IN THE MIDDLE, SENDING HIM CAREENING BACKWARD UNTIL HE TOO, FELL OUT THE WINDOW, SCREAMING AND GROWLING UNTIL HE LANDED WITH A THUNDEROUS CRASH.

"NO!" THE WOMAN BESIDE ALANA CRIED OUT HYSTERICALLY.

IT WAS HIS MOTHER'S CRY THAT BROUGHT LLEWELLYN BACK. HE CLOSED HIS EYES AND FELT THE CHANGE SLIP BACK OVER HIM. AS SOON AS IT DID, HE RUSHED AS QUICKLY AS HE COULD OVER TO THE WINDOW.

WHEN HE REACHED IT, HIS HEART STOPPED COLD AND HE STOOD STILL AS A STATUE.

THE DARKNESS REVEALED VERY LITTLE. BUT, ONE BEAM OF MOONLIGHT, UNFORTUNATELY PLACED, TOLD LLEW EVERYTHING HE NEEDED TO KNOW.

THERE, AMID THE DARK IVY AND NIGHT BLOOMING FLOWERS OF THE MANOR'S GARDEN LAY HIS BROTHER. DEAD.

www.ingramcontent.com/pod-product-compliance
Lightning Source LLC
LaVergne TN
LVHW041641070526
838199LV00053B/3500